You are the baby
that I was wishing for.
I can't imagine anyone
I could love *any* more.

There's nobody quite like you,
unique in every way...

From how you look and how you think,
to all the things you say.

You're just the perfect shape and the perfect size.

Your smile is the best smile,
your laugh is just right.

You were made for kisses
and cuddling tight.

And even when you're grumpy,
you're still my number one.

There's no one more important in this world to me.

And there is simply nothing that I would rather do . . .